There's a King in the Cupboard

There's a King in the Cupboard

Written by
Margaret Mahy

Illustrated by
Rosie Reeve

Orion
Children's Books

The King in the Cupboard originally appeared in
The Second Margaret Mahy Storybook
first published in Great Britain in 1973
by J.M. Dent & Sons
This abridged Early Reader edition
first published in Great Britain in 2015
by Orion Children's Books
an imprint of Hachette
Children's Group and published by
Hodder and Stoughton Limited
Orion House
5 Upper Saint Martin's Lane
London WC2H 9EA
An Hachette UK Company

1 3 5 7 9 10 8 6 4 2

The Orion Publishing Group's policy is to use papers that are
natural, renewable and recyclable products and made from wood
grown in sustainable forests.
The logging and manufacturing processes are expected to conform to
th environmental regulations of the country of origin.

A catalogue record for this book is available from the British Library.

ISBN 978 1 4440 1440 2

Printed and bound in China

www.orionbooks.co.uk

For Yumi

A family had once moved into
a different house.

9

It was just a small family –

a mum

a dad

and a little girl called Sarah.

Well, this house was not
exactly new – in fact it was one
of those big old houses full of
space and echoes.

Footsteps sounded loud and
doors shut like guns going off.

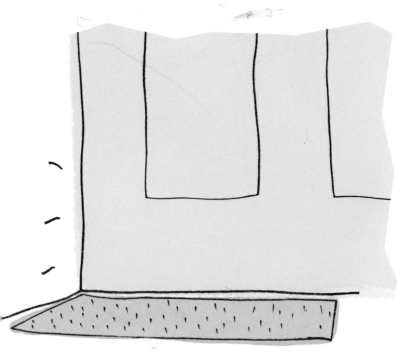

 The family were
all a bit nervous of
this different house,
and felt it was
always watching
and waiting to
surprise them.

Some of the furniture was inside and some was still coming along in the van, but the inside furniture looked nervous too, probably afraid that its people would go and leave it with no one to dust it.

Mum was making lunch when Sarah came and said, "Mummy, you know that big cupboard in the hall?"

"Yes," said her mum.

"Well, there's a king in it, Mummy. He's been shut in there for years and years."

"That's a shame," said Mum.
"Why doesn't he come out?"
"He can't!" said Sarah.

"He's enchanted. Spiders
have spun all over him,
Mummy."

"Poor king!" said Mum.

"Poor king!" repeated Sarah. Then she thought for a while and said, "Why don't you rescue him, Mummy?"

"I promise I would if I knew how to do it," Mum replied.

"I'll go and ask how," said Sarah and off she went.

Mum made some sandwiches and cut some cake before Sarah came back.

"You've just got to unlock the door and the king will come out," she told her mum.

"Is it locked?" asked
Mum, surprised.
"Then how do you know
there's a king in there?"
"I heard him
whispering to be let
out," Sarah said.

"He can only whisper and rustle. I tried to look through the keyhole, but it was too dark to see anything."

"All joking aside," said Mum, who did not believe in the king for one whispering, rustling moment, "I wonder if we have the key for that door."

She took up a key ring from
the bench and started looking
at the keys.

"This is for the
back door.

 This is for the
front door.

This is for the study
at the end of the hall."

"A witch enchanted the king," Sarah told her mum. "The king and his friends were just having a picnic when, **bang**, for no reason at all, this witch enchanted them.

Then she built a cupboard
round them. Then she built
a house round the cupboard.
And then that witch just stood
there laughing in a nasty way.

Have you found
the key?"
"No, there
doesn't seem to
be any key here,"
said Mum.

Sarah looked worried.

"There should be!" she cried.
"The king says today is the day
he is coming out."

But at that moment a blue
pigeon flew into the room.
It settled on the table and
dropped a tiny black key onto
the bread-and-butter plate.

Then it cooed and did a
dance, before it flew out of the
window again.

"I told you!" Sarah cried. "It's all working out. That's the key!"

"Well, what a thing to happen!" said Mum. "I wonder if it is the key to the cupboard."

As Mum jiggled the key in the lock, Sarah called, "Are you there, king? Are you listening? It won't be a moment now."

"I'm afraid the keyhole has rusted up," said Mum sadly. "The king will have to wait."

But at the very moment there came a small clinking and clanking, and four mice came down the hall dragging an oil can.

They dropped it at Sarah's
feet and ran back to their holes.

"That's useful," said Mum,
though she was frowning a bit
at the thought of mice in the
house.

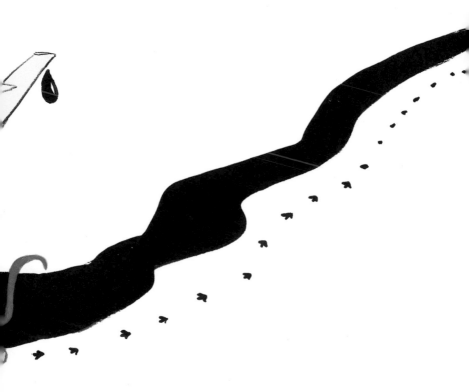

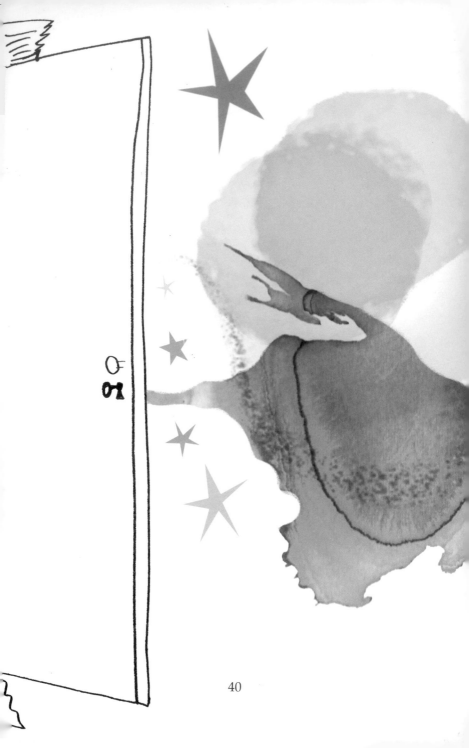

Mum picked up the oil can
and oiled the key and then the
keyhole.

The key turned easily.

Out from the cupboard
came a light like sunshine, the
smell of flowers and tomato
sandwiches and the sound of
drums and trumpets.

Out came not one, but seven
kings in purple and gold. Out
came a whole procession of
dancing people in green
dresses with flowers
in their hair. Out
came a whole herd
of silver deer,
strutting white
peacocks and
a pink
elephant
with a
rose tied to
its tail.

Last of all came a witch,
dragging a broom after her.

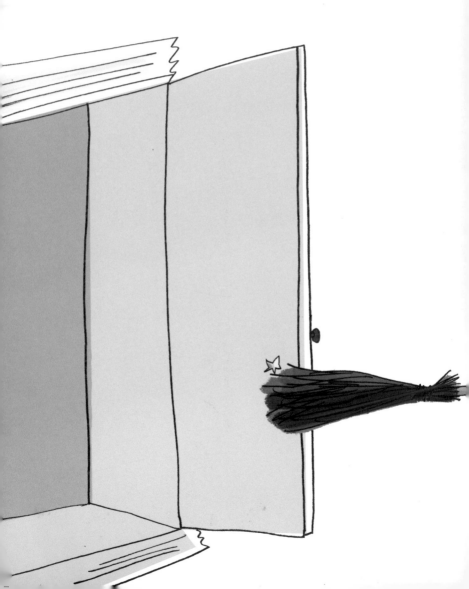

She looked at Sarah and her mum crossly.

"I enchanted myself into that cupboard by accident," she muttered. "A wrong word in the wrong place…"

The kings and the queens,
the green people, the silver deer,
the white peacocks, and the
pink elephant went down the
hall in a sort of parade and
a sort of dance.

They went one
step bumping
and one step
bouncing, out into
the lovely summer
day, off through the
overgrown garden
and then into
the trees. Their
colours shone,
flashed and
were lost.

The witch threw the broom
back into the cupboard.

"Get in there where you belong!" she snarled. "No more enchanting for me. I've had a change of heart."

She called to the kings, "Wait for me!" Then she went scuttling after them like a mud-coloured mouse.

Mum stared after her,
quite amazed.

After a moment she
opened the cupboard
door and peered in.

"There's just that broom left,"
she said.

But the broom went hopping
out, right down the hall, across
the garden and into the wood,
chasing after the witch and the
kings.

"Now it's empty," Sarah said happily. "It's good when enchantments work out properly and there's a happy ending."

From somewhere outside
came the echoes of trumpets
and drums as the kings of the
cupboard went on their way to
wherever they were going.

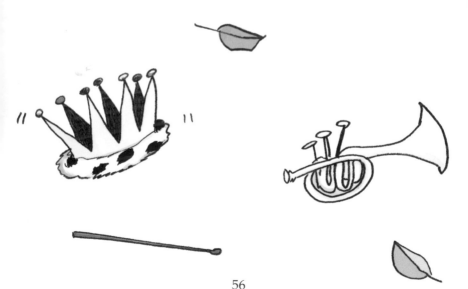

What are you going to read next?

Have more adventures with
Horrid Henry,

or save the day with Anthony Ant!

Become a superhero with Monstar,

float off to sea with Algy,

or have your very own Pirates' Picnic.

Grow carrots with

Lottie and Dottie,

make magic with
The Witch Dog,

and cast a
spell with

The Three
Little Magicians.

Enjoy all the Early Readers.

the orion star

CALLING ALL GROWN-UPS!
Sign up for the orion star newsletter to hear about your favourite authors and exclusive competitions, plus details of how children can join our 'Story Stars' review panel.

Sign up at:

www.orionbooks.co.uk/orionstar

Follow us 🐦 @the_orionstar
Find us f facebook.com/TheOrionStar